AN ADVENTURE AROUND IRELAND

IRELANDOPEDIA

A COMPENDIUM of MAPS, FACTS and KNOWLEDGE

THIS BOOK BELONGS TO

_____

FATTI and JOHN BURKE

GILL BOOKS

TeN WONDeRS OF IRELAND

PHOENIX PARK
Largest park
Co. Dublin

NEWGRANGE
Prehistoric monument
Co. Meath

CARRAUNTOOHIL
Highest point
Co. Kerry

THE BURREN
Limestone landscape
Co. Clare

RIVER SHANNON
Longest river
Co. Cavan – Co. Limerick

GIANT'S CAUSEWAY
Basalt columns
Co. Antrim

LOUGH NEAGH
Largest lake
Co. Antrim, Co. Armagh,
Co. Derry, Co. Down,
Co. Tyrone

BENBULBIN
Large rock formation
Co. Sligo

ROCK OF CASHEL
Complex of buildings
Co. Tipperary

SLIEVE LEAGUE
Tallest cliffs
Co. Donegal

ATLANTIC OCEAN

ULSTER

NORTH CHANNEL

DONEGAL

DERRY

ANTRIM

TYRONE

CONNACHT

LEITRIM

FERMANAGH

MONAGHAN

ARMAGH

DOWN

SLIGO

CAVAN

LOUTH

IRISH SEA

MAYO

ROSCOMMON

LONGFORD

WEST MEATH

MEATH

GALWAY

OFFALY

KILDARE

DUBLIN

LAOIS

WICKLOW

LEINSTER

CLARE

TIPPERARY

KILKENNY

CARLOW

WEXFORD

LIMERICK

KERRY

CORK

WATERFORD

MUNSTER

CELTIC SEA

CONTENTS

Welcome to
IRELANDOPEDIA!

Prepare to take a journey around Ireland and discover the wonders that lie just outside your door. There are 32 counties bursting with interesting people, extraordinary places and fascinating traditions all waiting for you to find.

Learn about haunted houses, unusual sports and odd festivals. Climb the tallest mountain, fish in the biggest lake and taste the local delicacies. With *Irelandopedia* you can become an expert on your home county or explore places you have never even heard of!

So make yourself cosy. You're about to find out what makes this little green island so special.

ROYAL CANAL

ÁRAS AN UACHTARÁIN is in the Phoenix Park. It is the official home of the President of Ireland.

PHOENIX PARK is one of the largest walled city parks in Europe. It's over 1,700 acres!

IRISH MUSEUM OF MODERN ART in Kilmainham has over 3,500 art works.

The original **LION** that appeared in the MGM logo was born in Dublin Zoo in 1919!

GLASNEVIN CEMETERY
contains the graves of many of Ireland's most prominent national figures.

The **FOUR COURTS** is Ireland's main courts building.

Dublin is home to many of Ireland's most famous **MUSICIANS**, like Thin Lizzy, U2 and The Dubliners!

Phil Lynott

Bono

Ronnie Drew

DUBLIN ZOO, in the Phoenix Park, is the largest zoo in Ireland. The 70-acre park is home to some 600 animals.

RIVER LIFFEY

GRAND CANAL

LEO BURDOCK'S opened in 1913, making it the oldest chipper in Ireland!

CHRIST CHURCH CATHEDRAL was founded in 1028. The heart of St Laurence O'Toole is in the Cathedral. It is said that the tomb of Strongbow is there also. You can see a mummified cat and rat in the crypt.

These odd vehicles can be spotted around Dublin. They are the Viking Splash Tour **AMPHIBIOUS VEHICLES** where you can learn about Dublin on the land and from the water!

GUINNESS STOREHOUSE is a Guinness-themed tourist attraction at St James's Gate Brewery.

GUINNESS

DUBLIN CITY
- - Baile Átha Cliath - -

JAMES JOYCE, the writer, was from Rathgar. He is well known for his books *Ulysses*, *Dubliners*, *Finnegans Wake* and lots of others.

DUBLIN IS THE CAPITAL CITY OF IRELAND

The National **BOTANIC GARDENS** are a beautiful flower-filled haven in Glasnevin. The gardens contain more than 15,000 plant species from around the world!

THE SPIRE is a 120-metre-high landmark in the heart of Dublin City.

The **MOLLY MALONE** statue is a tribute to the fishmonger who was commemorated in the song 'Cockles and Mussels', a Dublin anthem.

CROKE PARK, also known as *Croker*, is Ireland's National GAA Stadium. There's a GAA museum here too where you can learn the history of Irish sports.

BRAM STOKER, creator of *Dracula*, came from Clontarf.

O'CONNELL BRIDGE is thought to be the only bridge in Europe that is just as wide as it is long.

Poolbeg Towers

KEN DOHERTY, the snooker player, is from Ranelagh. He has been both world amateur and world professional champion.

DUBLIN CASTLE is a government complex of buildings, but was first built to defend Dublin City in the 13th century.

The remains of **ST VALENTINE** are buried in Whitefriar Street Church in Dublin City Centre.

The **AVIVA STADIUM** is where Ireland's football and rugby home games are played!

The **BOOK OF KELLS** can be seen in the library at Trinity College Dublin. It is a beautifully illustrated manuscript made in AD 800.

RTÉ

The headquarters of **RTÉ** are in Donnybrook. RTÉ produces Irish television, radio and internet shows!

OSCAR WILDE, the playwright, author and poet, was from Westland Row in the city centre.

THE DEAD ZOO is what Dubliners call the Natural History Museum. It has exhibitions of animals and insects from Ireland and around the world.

THE GIANT'S CAUSEWAY is made of 40,000 basalt columns from a lava flow. Legend says that Fionn Mac Cumhaill built the causeway so he could go to Scotland to fight a giant!

There is a myth that part of DUNLUCE CASTLE, including the kitchen, fell into the sea. Seven cooks were in it at the time and died. The castle is said to be haunted by them!

DULSE is often eaten in Antrim. Dulse is a type of purple edible seaweed.

CARRICKFERGUS has a fine medieval castle. There are dungeons beneath it where prisoners were kept.

Learn how to save our environment at the ECOS CENTRE in Ballymena.

JOEY DUNLOP, from Ballymoney, was a five-time World Motorcycle Champion!

Hollywood actor LIAM NEESON is from Ballymena.

YELLOWMAN is a hard, sticky, honeycomb toffee sold at the Auld Lammas Fair in August.

The musician VAN MORRISON was born in Belfast.

ANTRIM HILLS WALKING FESTIVAL takes place every October. Walkers are guided through the area's beautiful scenery.

C.S. LEWIS, the author of The Chronicles of Narnia, was born in Belfast.

There are nine GLENS in Antrim, each with their own special characteristics.

ANTRIM
Aontroim

There are more than 1,200 animals in BELFAST ZOO!

A car ferry goes from Larne to Stranraer and Cairnryan in **SCOTLAND**.

Carrick-a-Rede has a rope bridge that goes to *CARRICK ISLAND*. Some people who go to the island have to be rescued by boat because they are too scared to go back!

LOUGHAREEMA is a vanishing lake. This lake fills up during wet weather. In dry weather the water seeps down through the chalky ground and only the dry bed of the lake can be seen.

In **BUSHMILLS** they distil a world-famous whiskey.

GLENARIFF FOREST PARK is a nature reserve with beautiful waterfalls.

THE TITANIC was built in the Harland and Wolff shipyard.

The **POLLAN** is a freshwater whitefish found only in five Irish lakes, including Lough Neagh.

When **ST PATRICK** was a slave boy, he worked as a shepherd on Slemish Mountain.

↑ RIVER BANN

LOUGH NEAGH

City Hall

Belfast City Airport is named after **GEORGE BEST**, the famous footballer.

BELFAST is the capital city of Northern Ireland.

St Albert's Clock

The DeLorean

The **LAGAN CANAL**

Lough Neagh is the biggest lake in the British Isles. Fish found here include pollan, salmon, pike, brown trout and eels.

Lisburn was once the centre of the **LINEN** industry.

The Northern Ireland Assembly meets at **STORMONT**.

RIVER LAGAN

The Armagh Pipers Club organises an
UILLEANN PIPE FESTIVAL
every year to celebrate different
pipes from around the world.

LOUGH NEAGH

CONEY ISLAND
is a small, wooded island
on the Armagh side
of Lough Neagh.

BRIAN BORU
is said to be buried in the
St Patrick's Cathedral
graveyard in Armagh.

ARMAGH TOWN

Armagh is the only city in the
world with two cathedrals that
both have the same name –
ST PATRICK'S !

Lots of school tours go to
GOSFORD FOREST PARK
for nice walks and horse riding.
Sometimes you can see deer
there too!

Discover the mysteries
of the universe at Armagh
**PLANETARIUM
AND OBSERVATORY.**

**RIVER
BLACKWATER**

Armaghdown Bridge

Newry City Hall

The **APPLE BLOSSOM FESTIVAL**
takes place in May. It's a great opportunity
to try all the apple produce from the area.

About half of **NEWRY**
city is in Armagh and the other
half is in Down. It is one of
Ireland's oldest cities!

TAYTO CRISPS
are made in Tandragee for
the Northern Ireland market.
Tayto Castle tours are very
popular with young and old!

SLIEVE GULLION
is an extinct volcano. The
famous myth of Sétanta
and Culann's hound took
place here!

The **RING OF GULLION**
surrounds Slieve Gullion. It is a
'ring dyke' full of lovely walks and
beautiful scenery.

ARMAGH

Ard Mhacha

Armagh is known as 'The Orchard County' because of its many APPLE ORCHARDS.

BRAMLEY'S SEEDLING is the most popular apple grown in Armagh. They are used for cooking and making cider!

RIVER BANN

NAVAN CENTRE AND FORT is full of interesting stories about ancient Ireland. Here you can learn about how people lived way back in the Iron Age!

Poultry, dairy and beef are the main products of the Armagh FARMER.

A first edition of GULLIVER'S TRAVELS by Jonathan Swift can be seen in the Armagh City Library.

ROAD BOWLING is a popular pastime in Armagh.

THE NEWRY CANAL was the first summit canal built in Ireland or Great Britain! It links Lough Neagh and Carlingford Lough.

CARLINGFORD LOUGH

THE BARD OF ARMAGH is an old Irish ballad and the Bard of Armagh poetry competition takes place every November.

William McCrum, inventor of the PENALTY KICK in football, was from Armagh.

7

CARLOW
— Ceatharlach —

A visit to the floral **ALTAMONT GARDENS** is a magical experience!

Co. Carlow has a wonderful collection of **DOLMENS**. A dolmen is a megalithic tomb made of large rocks.

Three **METEORITES** fell to earth and landed in Leighlinbridge in 1999.

ÉIGSE CARLOW is an arts festival held every June.

PIERCE BUTLER of Tinryland was one of those who signed the American Constitution.

The Ireland rugby player **SEAN O'BRIEN** comes from Tullow.

The Carlow **AUTUMN WALKING FESTIVAL** is held in October.

Carlow's GAA nickname is **THE SCALLION EATERS**.

'That's a **PINK HORSE** of a different colour' is a Carlow phrase that means 'that's another thing altogether!'

RIVER BOATS bring visitors from New Ross to St Mullins.

There is a road in Myshall called the **CROPPY ROAD**. It was built by the United Irishmen after the 1798 rebellion.

CROPPY RD

RATHGALL is a large hillside fort and has the earliest Bronze Age workshop in Ireland.

The 100-ton capstone of **BROWNSHILL DOLMEN** is the largest in Europe!

There is a **MILITARY MUSEUM** outside Carlow Town which displays Irish Defence Forces uniforms from throughout history!

CARLOW TOWN

TULLOW agricultural show takes place every August. The show has been held here since 1946!

The River Slaney at Kildavin is one of the best places to see the very rare **GOOSANDER** and **YELLOWHAMMER**.

THE BATTLE OF CARLOW took place in 1798. There is a memorial in Graiguecullen to remember all those who died in the battle.

LEIGHLINBRIDGE CASTLE, also called Black Castle, was one of Ireland's first Norman forts.

MOUNT LEINSTER is the highest peak in the Blackstairs.

RIVER BARROW

JOHN TYNDALL, the physicist who explained why the sky is blue, was born in Leighlinbridge.

BLACKSTAIRS MOUNTAINS

ELVIS PRESLEY'S ancestor William Presley emigrated to America from Hacketstown 200 years ago!

The ancestors of **WALT DISNEY** are buried in Ballyloo!

The **GREAT SPOTTED WOODPECKER** has been seen in Kildavin. It only recently began breeding in Ireland!

RIVER SLANEY

The River Shannon leaves from the **SHANNON POT** on the side of the Cuilcagh Mountains. By jumping over the stream that leaves the 'Pot' you can boast that you jumped over the Shannon!

GAELIC FOOTBALL is the most popular sport in Cavan. Their team has won the Ulster Senior Football Championship more than any other county!

RIVER SHANNON

CUILCAGH MOUNTAINS

Cavan is known as **THE LAKELAND COUNTY** because it has over 360 lakes! Locals say there is 'a lake for every day of the year'.

There is a **CANOE CENTRE** in Carratraw. Young people love to take canoe lessons and go on nature tours there.

Marble Arch Caves Global **GEOPARK** has wonderful guided tours. You are shown through the caves on a boat.

LOUGH OUGHTER is a large complex of small lakes around the River Erne.

The **PIGHOUSE** Folk Museum is in Cornafean. It houses a collection of household objects and period clothing.

KILLYKEEN FOREST PARK is a great place to see Cavan's nature at its best.

CASTLE SAUNDERSON is an International Scouting Centre. This 30-acre site can cater for over 1,000 campers at any one time.

RIVER ERNE

CAVAN
— An Cabhán —

CAVAN CRYSTAL is Ireland's second biggest producer of Crystalware!

A **PORK FESTIVAL** is sometimes held in Ballyjamesduff. The *Olympigs* features racing pigs with woolen jockeys on their backs followed by a *Swine and Cheese* party!

POWERBOATING and water skiing are very popular activities on the Killeshandra Town Lake.

DRUMLANE monastic site is home to ruins of a church and a round tower from the year 555.

An Iron Age stone called the **CORLECK HEAD** was discovered in Drumeague. It is a carved stone with three smiling faces on it!

RIVER ANNALEE

CAVAN TOWN

Cootehill is a famous **FISHING** destination.

There is a Celtic pagan pilgrimage site at **MAGH SLÉCHT** near Kilnavert. There are groups of cairns, standing stones and burial sites.

Iron was produced in **SWANLINBAR** from the 17th to the 19th century.

Lough Oughter is a protected area for wildlife. Lots of **WHOOPER SWANS** spend winter here!

Lough Sheelin is Cavan's largest lake. It is home to birds such as the **GREAT CRESTED GREBE** and the **GOLDENEYE!**

LOUGH SHEELIN

LOUGH RAMOR

The singer **PERCY FRENCH** wrote a very popular song called 'Come Back Paddy Reilly to Ballyjamesduff' about his driver who left for Scotland. Paddy Reilly did come back and is buried there!

AILLWEE CAVE is in the heart of the Burren. You can take a stroll through the beautiful caverns, over chasms, under weird shapes and alongside a very loud waterfall. There is also a 'frozen' waterfall and the hibernation den of the extinct brown bear!

The BURREN is an extensive area of limestone that looks dramatic and strange. Its unusual environment means that arctic, Mediterranean *and* alpine plants can grow there!

THE CLIFFS OF MOHER are Ireland's most visited natural attraction. They stretch for 8km as the crow flies along the Clare coast.

JOHN PHILIP HOLLAND was an engineer from Clare who developed the first submarine to be formally commissioned by the US Navy. He is considered to be the father of the modern submarine.

MUTTON ISLAND

MUHAMMAD ALI, the heavyweight boxer, was made Freeman of Ennis. His great grandfather was from Co. Clare.

LOOP HEAD attracts thousands of tourists to the area. It has breath-taking scenic walks and stunning sea cliff views.

Shannon Dolphin and Wildlife Foundation is dedicated to the protection of the **SHANNON BOTTLENOSE DOLPHIN.**

DYSERT O'DEA is the restored 15th-century castle of the O'Dea clan. Today it houses the Clare Archaeology Centre.

SCATTERY ISLAND is home to the ruins of six churches and a very high round tower.

GALWAY BAY

CLARE
- An Clár -

LISDOONVARNA is known for its matchmakers. In September each year, one of Europe's largest matchmaking events is held in the town, attracting over 40,000 people looking for love.

Miltown Malbay is home to the annual **WILLIE CLANCY** Summer School and Festival. It is named after the famous uilleann piper.

Most of **FATHER TED** was filmed in Co. Clare. If you want to visit the Parochial House, it can be found in Lackareagh!

SLIEVE BERNAGH MOUNTAINS

LOUGH DERG

ENNIS

TORPEY HURLEYS are made in Sixmilebridge. They are the leading brand of hurleys in Ireland.

MICHAEL CUSACK, founder of the GAA, was born in Carron in 1847.

RIVER SHANNON

SHANNON AIRPORT has the longest runway in Ireland, at 3,199 metres!

BUNRATTY Castle & Folk Park is an authentic medieval fortress experience. It has a village where you can see different types of 19th-century houses, from tiny one-bedroom dwellings to a grand Georgian residence of the gentry.

THE CLARE SET is one of the most popular of Ireland's Set Dances.

DEER ISLAND

The **RIVER SHANNON** is Ireland's longest river. It flows into the Atlantic Ocean from the Shannon Estuary.

SONIA O'SULLIVAN was born in Cobh. She was one of the world's leading female runners. She won a silver medal in the 2000 Olympics!

2000

MULLAGHAREIRK MOUNTAINS

MIDLETON is where lots of famous Irish whiskeys are distilled, like Powers, Jameson and Paddy. It has the world's biggest pot still for making whiskey!

The shortest St Patrick's Day parade in the world takes place in **DRIPSEY**!

RIVER BLACKWATER

ROY KEANE has played football for both Manchester United and the Republic of Ireland.

The **MUSKERRY** Gaeltacht is one of two Irish-speaking regions in Cork.

Fota Island in Cork Harbour is home to **FOTA WILDLIFE PARK** which is the only wildlife park in Ireland. It is home to nearly 30 mammal species like red pandas, cheetahs and giraffes.

DERRYNASAGGART MOUNTAINS

RIVER LEE

The Cork **JAZZ FESTIVAL** takes place each October.

CAHA MOUNTAINS

The nationalist leader **MICHAEL COLLINS** was from Clonakilty.

SIR WALTER RALEIGH is said to have planted the first potato in Ireland in Youghal around 1588.

BANTRY BAY

SLIEVE MISKISH

CAPE CLEAR ISLAND is one of two Gaeltachts in Cork.

There is a model **RAILWAY VILLAGE** in Clonakilty.

People in Cork love to eat **TRIPE AND DRISHEEN.** Tripe is the lining of the stomach of a sheep or cow and drisheen is a type of blood sausage.

BOY

People in Cork are known for saying the words 'LIKE' AND 'BOY' at the end of their sentences, like!

LIKE

BALLYMALOE has a famous restaurant and cookery school run by the Allen family. They started making their well-known tomato relish there too!

MALLOW is home to Cork's only horse-racing course.

There are **29 BRIDGES** in Cork city!

BOGGERAGH MOUNTAINS

ST COLMAN'S CATHEDRAL has a 49-bell carillon, the largest in Ireland and the UK!

By kissing the **BLARNEY STONE** at Blarney Castle, it is claimed that you can receive the 'Gift of the Gab'.

CORK CITY

THE ENGLISH MARKET in Cork city is one of the best and oldest food markets in the world.

CORK HARBOUR

RIVER BANDON

COBH lies in the centre of Cork harbour. This was the last port of call for the Titanic.

The **BALLINCOLLIG** Royal Gunpowder Mills made gunpowder that was used by the British in the wars with Napoleon. Today it is a museum and visitor centre.

Common and grey **SEALS** can be seen along the coast.

There is a fun holiday village in **TRABOLGAN.**

CORK
Corcaigh

The 1960s saw Derry become the focus of the **CIVIL RIGHTS** movement in Northern Ireland.

ONE MAN ONE VOTE

JOBS NOT CREED

BENONE STRAND is Ireland's longest beach. It is 7 miles of wide-open sand and sea. People love to go on holiday here.

RIVER FOYLE

LOUGH FOYLE

AUSTINS in Derry city is the world's oldest independent department store!

The lovely **MUSSENDEN TEMPLE** is a symbol of Derry.

DERRY CITY

The **DERRY PEACE BRIDGE** is a powerful symbol of peace.

The city of Derry has a number of **DIFFERENT NAMES**. It is known as Londonderry, Derry and Stroke City.

The 17th-century **WALLS** that encircle the old city centre make Derry the most complete walled city in Europe.

SPERRIN MOUNTAINS

The Burntollet River flows over the highest waterfalls in Northern Ireland in the deciduous **BANAGHER FOREST**

The highest point in the county is the summit of **SAWEL MOUNTAIN**.

MILK OF MAGNESIA was invented in Derry by Sir James Murray in 1817.

MILK OF MAGNESIA

AMELIA EARHART landed in farmland just outside Derry city on her solo transatlantic flight.

DERRY

Doire

PORTSTEWART STRAND is very popular with surfers.

all kinds of everything...

Derry is nicknamed the **OAK LEAF COUNTY** because the Irish name *Doire* translates as *oak grove*.

DANA, who was Ireland's first Eurovision winner, is from Derry. She went on to become a member of the European Parliament.

SHIRT-MAKING was one of the city's main industries. In 1902 there were 38 shirt factories in Derry!

River Bann

SHEEP AND COWS are reared in the Sperrin uplands while potatoes and cereals are grown in the fertile lowlands.

The ruins of **DUNGIVEN PRIORY** used to be a Celtic monastery. It was founded by St Nechtan in the 7th century.

St Columb's College is the only secondary school in the world to produce two Nobel Prize winners – **JOHN HUME** (Peace) **AND SEAMUS HEANEY** (Literature)

GOLD was discovered in the Sperrin Mountains and mining has been carried out there since 2007.

LOUGH NEAGH

DONEGAL
Dún na nGall

TORY ISLAND is the only place in Ireland that still has its own king! The current king is Patsy Dan Rodgers.

LETTERKENNY is the biggest town in Donegal. It is sometimes referred to as the Cathedral Town.

The **WISHING STONE** on Tory Island is said to grant your wish if you have the nerve to step onto it or if you can throw three stones on top of it.

ARRANMORE is one of two permanently inhabited islands in Donegal. Over 500 people live there and most of them are Irish speakers.

Market Square

CLOUGHANEELY

GWEEDORE

BUNBEG

THE ROSSES

MOUNT ERRIGAL is the highest peak in Donegal.

BUNBEG has one of the smallest fishing harbours in the world!

DERRYVEAGH MOUNTAINS

The Ballyshannon **FOLK FESTIVAL** is held on the August bank holiday weekend each year.

The Rosses Gaeltacht has over 130 **LAKES**!

The **SLIEVE LEAGUE** cliffs are the sixth-highest sea cliffs in Europe!

BLUESTACK MOUNTAINS

KILLYBEGS is the largest fishing port in Ireland! In the summer there is a street festival celebrating all the fish that were caught that year.

LOUGH ERNE

BUNDORAN is a popular seaside resort. People from all over the world travel there to go surfing!

RIVER ERNE

Three peninsulas of great beauty are **ROSGUILL, FANAD AND INISHOWEN**

MALIN HEAD is the most northerly point of the island of Ireland.

MOVILLE has Europe's biggest Bob Dylan music festival each year – DylanFest.

LOUGH SWILLY

Pole Star Monument

RIVER FOYLE

LOUGH FOYLE

THE FLIGHT OF THE EARLS Heritage Centre in Rathmullan tells the story of the rebels Hugh O'Neill and Rory O'Donnell, who fled Ireland in 1607.

LIFFORD is the capital of the county and the seat of Donegal County Council.

AUL DOLL

In Donegal, if someone is speaking about their **AUL DOLL**, they're referring to their mother!

GLENVEAGH National Park is one of the largest national parks in Ireland, located on 16,000 acres of mountainside.

RIVER FINN

DANIEL O'DONNELL, the singer, grew up in Kincasslagh.

McDAID'S FOOTBALL SPECIAL is a Donegal delicacy. It is a fizzy drink made with a mix of seven secret flavours.

GOLDEN EAGLES can be seen around Glenveagh National Park.

Donegal's county slogan is **'UP HERE IT'S DIFFERENT'.**

RORY GALLAGHER, the guitarist and songwriter, was born in Ballyshannon. There is even a statue of him there!

DOWN
— An Dún —

DAVID TRIMBLE, the former Ulster Unionist leader, was born in Bangor.

BELFAST CITY is mostly in Co. Antrim but parts of east and south Belfast are in Co. Down.

HARRY FeRGUSON, the inventor of the tractor, was born near Dromore.

RORY McILROY, the world number one golfer, is from Holywood in Co. Down.

RIVER BANN

VeDA is a dark malted bread special to Northern Ireland. It is different from the north England Veda, which is sticky and much sweeter.

BALLYCOPELAND WINDMILL is a fully working windmill, the only one of its kind in the county.

JANE EYRE
CHARLOTTE BRONTE

James Martin, the inventor of the **EjeCTION SEAT,** was born in Crossgar.

HOT CHOCOLATE was first invented by Sir Hans Sloane from Killyleagh.

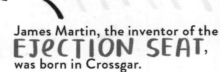

MOUNT STeWART near Newtownards has one of the most beautiful gardens in the world.

EDDIe IRVINe, the Formula One driver with Jordan and Ferrari, was born in Newtownards.

The DeLorean

BELFAST LOUGH

BELFAST

THE OLD INN
in Crawfordsburn is one of Ireland's oldest hotels, with records dating back to 1614.

City Hall

STRANGFORD LOUGH

RIVER LAGAN

THE DOWN ROYAL RACECOURSE
is in Lisburn, on the border of Down and Antrim.

KILLYLEAGH CASTLE
is the oldest occupied castle in Ireland. Built in the 12th century, it is still in use as a private home.

SLIEVE CROOB
is the source of the River Lagan.

ARDS PENINSULA

LEGANANNY DOLMEN
is a well-known megalithic tomb. It is 4,500 years old!

WUTHERING HEIGHTS
EMILY BRONTE

TOLLYMORE FOREST PARK
features the Tollymore National Outdoor Centre, which is the Northern Ireland Centre for Mountaineering and Canoeing.

DOWNPATRICK

PATRICK BRONTË,
the father of Anne, Emily, Charlotte and Branwell, was born near Banbridge.

Portaferry, on the Ards Peninsula, is home to EXPLORIS – the Northern Ireland Aquarium.

SLIEVE DONARD
is the highest peak in Northern Ireland.

In Down, people sometimes call ice cream cones a
'POKE'

MOURNE MOUNTAINS

SILENT VALLEY RESERVOIR
is in the Mourne Mountains. It supplies most of the water for Co. Down and most of Belfast.

DUNDONALD LEISURE PARK
has an Olympic size ice rink! The Belfast Giants ice hockey team train there.

CARLINGFORD LOUGH

CONOR MCGREGOR, the mixed martial artist, was born in Dublin.

The **KEY CROPS** from Co. Dublin include mushrooms, potatoes, cauliflower, strawberries, flowers, bulbs and Christmas trees!

SKERRIES is a fishing village which is home to two windmills and a watermill.

NAUL HILLS

The singer-songwriter **SINÉAD O'CONNOR** was born in Glenageary. She is best known for her song 'Nothing Compares 2 U'.

The **DALKEY BOOK FESTIVAL** is held in June every year. Maeve Binchy and Hugh Leonard are two writers from Dalkey.

The National Aquatic Centre in **BLANCHARDSTOWN** is Ireland's principal facility for water sports and forms part of the national sports campus.

SWORDS dates back to AD 560 when it was founded by St Colmcille. The round tower is also an indicator of early Christian settlement.

HOWTH HEAD

ROYAL CANAL

RIVER LIFFEY

GRAND CANAL

DUBLIN CITY

DUBLIN AIRPORT is the busiest airport in Ireland!

DÚN LAOGHAIRE is one of Ireland's major passenger ferry ports and yachting centres.

CLONDALKIN has an 8th-century round tower. It is one of the oldest and best preserved in the country.

The **WILDLIFE** in the Dublin Mountains includes red squirrel, red grouse, kestrel, jay and sika deer.

THE DUBLIN MOUNTAINS are really hills! They are part of the Wicklow range on the Dublin boundary.

KIPPURE is the highest mountain in Co. Dublin. It is also the source of the River Liffey.

Lead open-cast mining began around 1807 on the western side of **CARRICKGOLLOGAN**.

ROCKABILL
is a group of two islands, The Rock and The Bill. Rockabill has the largest colony of roseate terns in Europe.

DUBLIN
Baile Átha Cliath

JOHN M. SYNGE, the playwright, was born in Rathfarnham. He wrote *The Playboy of the Western World* and is a founder of the Abbey Theatre in Dublin City.

BOSCO

The **LAMBERT PUPPET THEATRE** is in Monkstown. It used to produce children's television series on RTÉ like *Bosco* and *Wanderly Wagon*.

LAMBAY ISLAND
was the landing site of the winners of the 1921 Gordon Bennett Gas Balloon Race.

MALAHIDE
has a wonderful castle with secret gardens, a museum, an exhibition of Irish history and lots more.

BAILY LIGHTHOUSE
is located on the southeastern part of Howth Head.

DAMIEN DUFF
was born in Rathfarnham. He has played football for Newcastle United, Chelsea, Fulham, Blackburn Rovers and the Republic of Ireland.

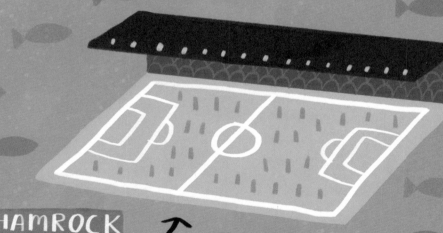

SHAMROCK ROVERS
football club play their home games in Tallaght Stadium.

THE FORTY FOOT
in Sandycove was once a *men's only* bathing place but it is open to everyone now.

The first **LIFEBOAT STATION** in Ireland was established in Sandycove in 1803.

Large flights of **WILD GEESE** and swans visit Lough Erne in late autumn.

The **GILLAROO** is a variety of trout that is only found in Lough Melvin!

BOA ISLAND is the largest island in Lough Erne. It is connected to the mainland by two bridges.

LOUGH ERNE

BELLEEK POTTERY produces the world famous Belleek fine parian china. It is a traditional wedding gift.

LOUGH MELVIN

There is a Classic **FISHING** Festival based around Enniskillen in mid-May.

THE KINGFISHER CYCLE TRAIL was the first long-distance cycle trail in Ireland, through the counties of Fermanagh, Leitrim, Cavan, Donegal and Monaghan.

In Florence Court Forest Park there is a famous **YEW** tree, said to be the parent of all the Irish yew trees.

BIG DOG FOREST is 1,000 hectares in size and is covered mainly with conifers. The star attractions are the two hills known as Big Dog and Little Dog. They are said to be Fionn Mac Cumhail's Irish wolfhounds who were turned into mountains by a witch whom they chased!

Marble Arch Caves Global **GEOPARK** has some of the finest show caves in Europe. The Geopark covers the mountains and lowlands of both Fermanagh *and* Cavan.

BENAUGHLIN MOUNTAIN is in the Cuilcagh Mountain range. The name means 'Peak of the Speaking Horse'.

Some people believed that the horse of the **KING OF THE FAIRIES** would appear on the last Sunday of July to talk to local people.

Marble Arch was home to the now extinct **GIANT IRISH DEER**, a complete skeleton of which can be found in the National Museum of Natural History.

FERMANAGH

Fear Manach

Co. Fermanagh is largely rural and agricultural, with the main industry here being **LIVESTOCK**, including sheep, cattle and pigs.

There are many **ISLANDS** on Lough Erne – 109 in the lower lake and 90 in the upper.

BALLINAMALLARD is a pretty village that has won several best kept village awards.

The **LADY OF THE LAKE** is a mythical figure who is said to appear gliding over the waters of Lower Lough Erne wearing a blue dress and holding flowers. The Lady is said to be an omen of good times to come!

ENNISKILLEN is the county town situated on an island between Fermanagh's two major lakes. Enniskillen Castle was built by the Maguires in the 16th century and has two museums!

RIVER ERNE

HEADHUNTERS Barber Shop & Railway Museum in Enniskillen has a large collection of Irish railway memorabilia on display. Enjoy this while they cut your hair!

O'Doherty's Fine Meats of Enniskillen are the makers of the award-winning Fermanagh delicacy, **BLACK BACON**.

LOUGH ERNE

The JUNGLE BOOK

CROM ESTATE is one of Ireland's most important nature conservation areas. Wild deer, pine marten and all eight species of native bats can be seen here.

The **BALLINAMORE AND BALLYCONNELL CANAL** links Upper Lough Erne to the River Shannon, which makes it popular with boaters and anglers.

REV. JAMES McDONALD of Ballinamallard was an ancestor of Rudyard Kipling (author of *The Jungle Book*), Stanley Baldwin (former English Prime Minister) and the artist Sir Edward Burne-Jones.

The actor PETER O'TOOLE was born in Connemara. He is best known for his role in *Lawrence of Arabia*.

TERRYLAND Forest Park is an urban forest park in Galway. It's great for spotting mammals like foxes and otters!

INISHBOFIN

LOUGH MASK

BENBAUN is one of the Twelve Bens and is the highest peak in Galway.

CLIFDEN in west Galway is where Alcock and Brown landed after the world's first transatlantic flight.

LOUGH CORRIB

The TWELVE BENS is a mountain range in Connemara.

CONNEMARA is Ireland's largest Gaeltacht region.

ROS NA RÚN

SPIDDAL is a seaside village and is the setting for the TG4 soap *Ros na Rún*.

KYLEMORE ABBEY was founded as a convent for nuns who fled Belgium in World War I. The estate includes beautiful walled gardens that are a lovely place for nature walks!

The KING'S HEAD pub in Galway City was once owned by the man who was chosen by Oliver Cromwell to execute King Charles I.

The CONNEMARA PONY Show in August is a celebration of this world-famous breed of pony.

The heaviest DUCK EGG in the world was laid in Tuam. It weighed 227g!

GALWAY BAY

INIS MÓR

INIS MEÁIN

INIS OÍRR

The ARAN ISLANDS are located in Galway Bay.

Kinvara has a beautiful harbour that has a festival for GALWAY HOOKER boats each year.

GALWAY

Gaillimh

ARAN SWEATERS are special to this area and are popular all over Ireland.

The **CLADDAGH RING** is a traditional Irish ring which represents love, loyalty and friendship.

RIVER SUCK

ATHENRY
is one of the most notable medieval walled towns in Ireland. The song 'The Fields of Athenry' is about this area.

See a dog's bones in **PORTUMNA CASTLE**. Long ago, a child fell out of the upper window of the castle. But an Irish wolfhound called Fury ran and broke the child's fall and saved it. When the dog died it was buried there.

ST JARLATH'S WHEEL
is the symbol of Tuam. The wheel of St Jarlath's chariot broke and he believed that it was a sign that this was the place he would die. So he founded his famous monastery there!

RIVER CORRIB

The Clarenbridge **OYSTER** Festival is held in September. People come from abroad to taste the delicious oysters.

GALWAY CITY

THOOR BALLYLEE was the home of W.B. Yeats.

RIVER SHANNON

COOLE PARK
was the home of Lady Gregory, a founder of the Abbey Theatre. It is a nature reserve that contains the famous Autograph Tree.

THE SLIEVE AUGHTY MOUNTAINS
spread from Galway into Clare.

CHRISTOPHER COLUMBUS
visited Galway 15 years before he discovered America.

LOUGH DERG

The **TUROE STONE** is 1.68 metres high and is one of the finest examples of Iron Age art in Europe. It is decorated with spirals, circles, curves and other motifs.

KeRRy
Ciarraí

BLeNNeRVILLe WINDMILL is the tallest tower mill in Europe. The windmill was used for grinding corn.

A number of books were written by natives of the **BLASKeT ISLANDS** that record their way of life, such as the famous *Peig* by Peig Sayers.

THE ROSE OF TRALEe is one of Ireland's largest festivals. It involves selected women from Irish communities throughout the world in a competition to select the Rose of Tralee for that year.

The Ballybunion Wild Atlantic **SEAWEED WEEKEND** celebrates everything you can do with seaweed, like using it for cookery, beauty products and baths.

TRALEE

BLASKeT ISLANDS

MOUNT BRANDON is popular with pilgrims. The path to the peak is marked by small white crosses and the peak itself is topped by a large metal cross.

The **PUCK FAIR** in Killorglin is one of Ireland's oldest festivals. A mountain goat is crowned king and rules over the town for three days before being released back on the mountain.

CORCA DHUIBHNE Gaeltacht is situated on the Dingle Peninsula.

DINGLe is home to Fungie the dolphin!

RIVER LAUNE

LOUGH LEANE

CARRAUNTOOHIL is the highest peak in Ireland. It is 1,038 metres high and is the central peak of the Macgillycuddy's Reeks range.

UPPER LAKE

MUCKROSS LAKE

There is a **KING SCALLOP** festival on Valentia Island every year to celebrate Kerry's delicious scallops!

UÍBH RÁTHACH Gaeltacht is situated on the Iveragh Peninsula.

MACGILLYCUDDY'S REEKS

VALENTIA ISLAND

THE CONOR PASS is the highest mountain pass in Ireland and provides wonderful views from the road.

GALLARUS ORATORY is a unique structure that looks like an upturned boat and is made of stone. It's still waterproof although it was built over 1,000 years ago!

RIVER ROUGHTY

THE SKELLIG ISLANDS are home to hundreds of seabirds such as gannet, puffin, cormorant, shag, razorbill, guillemot and many varieties of gull.

385-million-year-old fossilised **TETRAPOD** footprints were discovered on the north coast of Valentia Island in 1993. A tetrapod is a four-limbed vertebrate such as a newt or lizard.

DANIEL O'CONNELL was a leader of the Irish people. He helped achieve Catholic Emancipation and later appeared on the Irish £20.

The **CHARLIE CHAPLIN** Comedy Film Festival is held each year in Waterville. Chaplin spent many summers here with his family.

£20

The lovely **KERRY BLUE TERRIER** is an Irish breed, which originated in the 18th century. They are good dogs for hunting and guarding your home.

TORC WATERFALL, approximately 22 metres high, and the Owengarriff River which feeds it rises in the Devil's Punchbowl (a lake) on nearby Mangerton Mountain.

MÍCHEÁL Ó MUIRCHEARTAIGH, the Gaelic games commentator, is from Dún Síon. He is known as the 'voice of Gaelic games'.

JOHN B. KEANE was a playwright, novelist and essayist from Listowel, Co. Kerry. His play *The Field* was made into a successful film.

The **FAHAN BEEHIVE HUTS** are situated to the west of Dingle. Only four remain out of a settlement of 400.

People like to see **KILLARNEY NATIONAL PARK** by jaunting car. These can be hired in Killarney. The drivers are called jarveys.

TOM CREAN, nicknamed the 'Irish Giant', was an Irish seaman and Antarctic explorer from Annascaul.

CRAG CAVE near Castleisland is filled with spectacular stalagmites and stalactites.

RIVER BOYNE

ROYAL CANAL

Leinster's largest **HEDGE MAZE** is a fabulous attraction. It is just outside Prosperous.

MONDELLO PARK in Caragh is Ireland's only international motorsport venue.

GRAND CANAL

THE BOG OF ALLEN is a large raised bog. The Bog of Allen Nature Centre is an international centre for peatland education, conservation and research.

In legends, the *Fianna* used to meet at the **HILL OF ALLEN**.

NAAS

The highest point in Kildare is **CUPIDSTOWN HILL**.

NAAS is the county town of Kildare. It is the centre of the horse-racing industry with two racecourses: Naas and Punchestown.

RIVER BARROW

The **JAPANESE GARDENS** that symbolise the 'Life of Man' are situated in the grounds of the Irish National Stud farm. They are regarded as the finest of their kind in Europe.

BOG BUTTER, coins and an ancient dugout canoe are just some of the things that have been recovered from the Bog of Allen.

The folk singer **CHRISTY MOORE** is from Kildare!

NEWBRIDGE SILVERWARE is a company that designs and manufactures cutlery, jewellery and giftware.

The Curragh has its own **MILITARY MUSEUM**! The museum is subdivided into three parts: the environment, the British military presence and the Irish Defence Forces.

Athy Heritage Centre has a permanent exhibition devoted to explorer **SIR ERNEST SHACKLETON**. It has an original sledge and harness from one of his Antarctic expeditions on display!

KILDARE
Cill Dara

RIVER LIFFEY

ST BRIGID founded a double monastery and was Abbess of the convent, the first in Ireland. Around it grew the town of Kildare.

MAYNOOTH CASTLE was founded in the early 13th century and became the principal home of the Kildare branch of the Geraldines, or the FitzGerald dynasty.

DONNELLY'S HOLLOW is the site of a famous boxing match that was held in 1815 between Dan Donnelly of Ireland and George Cooper of England. Dan Donnelly's right arm is preserved and kept in Kilcullen.

Because the River Barrow and the Barrow Line canal go through it, Monasterevin has a lot of bridges. It is sometimes referred to as the **VENICE OF IRELAND.**

THE WONDERFUL BARN is a strange, corkscrew-shaped barn built on the Leixlip side of Castletown House Estate. It was built to store grain.

MOONE village has a famous high cross and the remains of a church that is believed to have been founded by St Columba.

POLLARDSTOWN FEN National Nature Reserve is 3 km west of Newbridge. In the summer you can see mute swans, herons, little grebes, coot and moorhen on the lake.

THE IVERK SHOW
in Piltown is the longest running Agricultural Show in Ireland, having been founded in 1826.

The **CAT LAUGHS** Comedy Festival takes place in Kilkenny annually.

Callan is the birthplace of **EDMUND RICE**, founder of the Christian Brothers.

Kilkenny people are nicknamed **THE CATS**.

Ireland's only **REPTILE ZOO** is in Gowran.

JAMES HOBAN
from Cuffesgrange was the architect who designed the White House in Washington, D.C.

Freshford hosts the annual **IRISH CONKER CHAMPIONSHIPS**. The chestnuts for the competition are provided by 52 horse chestnut trees that surround the village green.

KILKENNY CASTLE
was built for William Marshal, the 4th Earl of Pembroke, c. 1146–1219. You can take a tour of Kilkenny Castle and city on a train. It is called the Castle Express.

KILKENNY
-Cill Chainnigh-

Kyteler's Inn is where Dame Alice Kyteler was born in the late 1200s. She was accused of being a **WITCH** but she fled Ireland and her maid was burned at the stake instead. Her ghost is said to haunt the streets to this day!

JENKINSTOWN PARK is home to stoats, pheasant, ravens and the long-eared owl!

ROTHE HOUSE is the only example of an early 17th-century merchant's townhouse in Ireland.

JERPOINT ABBEY is an outstanding Cistercian abbey founded in the second half of the 12th century. Today it is a well maintained ruin.

KILKENNY CITY

RIVER NORE

KNOCKROE Passage Tomb is located in a lovely setting on the slopes above the Lingaun River. The site dates to around 3,000 BC.

BRANDON HILL is Kilkenny's highest point.

MILK

GLANBIA, the dairy manufacturer, has its headquarters on the edge of Kilkenny city.

WOODSTOCK GARDENS in Inistioge has 50 acres of beautiful woodland and lakes.

Castlecomer has a great attraction called the **TREE TOP** Adventure Walk. You can walk high up through the trees on rope walkways!

Kilkenny have won more **ALL-IRELAND** Finals than any other county!

RIVER BARROW

HENRY SHEFFLIN, the greatest hurler of modern times, comes from Ballyhale.

RIVER SUIR

LAOIS
Laois

MOUNTMELLICK was famous for its lace. It is the home of a unique textile art which is a beautiful white-on-white embroidery technique.

A beautiful POET'S COTTAGE in Camross gives one an idea of what life was like for people in rural Ireland in the 1800s.

The SLIEVE BLOOM MOUNTAINS are one of the oldest mountain ranges in Europe.

RIVER NORE

DARINA ALLEN, the chef and food writer, was born in Cullohill.

One of the highlights of the year in Durrow is the annual SCARECROW FESTIVAL. Here you can learn butter making, hurley making and scarecrow making!

FLORA of the Slieve Bloom Mountains include fly agaric mushrooms, wild orchids and bog asphodel.

WILLIAM RUSSELL GRACE, from Ballylinan, was the Mayor of New York and founded W.R. Grace and Co., the chemical company.

Donaghmore Famine WORKHOUSE MUSEUM tells the story of the families who lived and died within the Famine Workhouse walls during the Great Famine.

There is a **FRENCH FESTIVAL** every July in Portarlington. They have street theatre, a market village, French food and wine tasting, and a world snail-eating competition.

RIVER BARROW

Laois is doubly **LAND-LOCKED**. It is the only county in Ireland that doesn't have a neighbour that touches the sea.

AN CNOC BÁN is a working organic farm in Spink.

PORTLAOISE

Stradbally Estate offers many attractions, the biggest being **ELECTRIC PICNIC**, a music festival held every summer.

TREASURE is said to be buried beneath the Rock of Dunamase but is guarded by Bandog, a huge Mastiff with gaping fiery jaws.

Portlaoise is home to the **IRISH FLY FISHING AND GAME SHOOTING** Museum. This is a treat for anyone interested in country life.

St Mochua founded a monastery in **TIMAHOE**. The round tower has an extraordinary carved doorway making it the most elegant round tower in Ireland.

The National **STEAM RALLY** in Stradbally is the oldest steam rally in Ireland. There is also a Steam Museum with permanent exhibits.

ABBEYLEIX Heritage House is a visitor centre which houses a museum and model railway.

Leitrim has the **SHORTEST COASTLINE** of any county in Ireland. It is only 3 km long!

A cairn on **TRUSKMORE** Mountain marks the highest point of the county.

When the waters of Lough Allen are low, you can see the remains of **CRANNOGS**. These were used from the Bronze Age right up to the Middle Ages.

POLL NA MBÉAR (Cave of the Bears) at Glenade is where some of the best preserved examples of Irish brown bear bones were discovered by cavers in 1997.

DARTRY MOUNTAINS

There are a variety of **ALPINE AND ARCTIC PLANTS** in the Dartry Mountains, like alpine saxifrage, chickweed willowherb and alpine bistort.

LOUGH GILL

The **MANORHAMILTON CASTLE** and Heritage Centre has a permanent exhibition and offers guided tours of the castle ruins and grounds.

The Costello Memorial **CHURCH** is the smallest chapel in Ireland and reputedly the second smallest chapel in the world. It was built in the 19th century by Edward Costello for his late wife, Mary Josephine.

LOUGH ALLEN

CARRICK-ON-SHANNON

GLENCAR WATERFALL is only 15 metres high but very beautiful. William Butler Yeats mentioned it in his poem, 'The Stolen Child'.

Rossinver has an **ORGANIC CENTRE** which features demonstration gardens with a heritage garden, a children's garden, a taste garden, a willow sculpture area, poultry and more.

RIVER SHANNON

The National **ASTRONOMY** Centre was built to look like a ruined tower to fit into the landscape. Construction began in 2001 but money ran out and the stone tower was left empty. The site now belongs to the Department of Agriculture, Food and the Marine.

LEITRIM
— Liatroim —

GLENVIEW FOLK MUSEUM
has a collection of more than 6,000 antique items ranging from pre-Famine Ireland to the recent past.

The soil of Co. Leitrim is particularly water retentive and so people joke that land in the county is sold by the **GALLON** rather than by the acre.

The **LEITRIM DESIGN HOUSE** in Carrick-on-Shannon is a showcase of Irish craft and design, like glass, metal, ceramics, wood and photography.

MARGARET HAUGHERY
was born in Carrigallen. She moved to New Orleans in the 19th century and opened four orphanages there. She was referred to as the 'Angel of the Delta' and 'Mother of Orphans'.

In the area around Lough Melvin, the endangered **GLOBEFLOWER** can be seen.

The highest concentration of **SWEATHOUSES** in Ireland can be found around Lough Allen. Sweathouses were buildings that worked like saunas. The heat inside the buildings was thought to relieve the patients' symptoms.

Leitrim people often say **'THIS IS ME, IS THAT YOU?'** when answering the phone!

LIMERICK
Luimneach

Limerick-born **MICHAEL D. HIGGINS,** the ninth president of Ireland, is a politician, poet, sociologist and author.

THE HUNT MUSEUM in Limerick city has one of Ireland's greatest private collections of art and antiquities. It includes art by Renoir, Picasso and Yeats.

FRANK McCOURT is from Limerick, and his popular book *Angela's Ashes* was set in the city.

ANGELA'S ASHES

FRANK MCCOURT

DAIRYING and beef rearing account for most of the farming activity in Co. Limerick.

ADARE has been called Ireland's prettiest village!

THE BRIDGE OF TEARS in Newcastle West was a famous last farewell point when people were leaving on a carriage to Cork before emigrating to North America.

MULLAGHAREIRK MOUNTAINS

KING JOHN'S CASTLE is situated on King's Island in the heart of medieval Limerick City. Its exhibitions bring to life over 800 years of local history.

LIMERICK CITY

SLIEVE FELIM MOUNTAINS

TERRY WOGAN, the television and radio presenter, was born in Limerick.

THOMOND PARK is the home ground of Munster Rugby, one of the most successful and best supported rugby clubs in the world.

LOUGH GUR

The Jim Kemmy Municipal Museum contains a wide range of exhibits. One artefact is a nail, a pedestal on which merchants paid their debts, giving rise to the expression **PAYING ON THE NAIL**.

Lough Gur is home to the largest **STONE CIRCLE** in Ireland!

Thomas Fitzgerald came from Bruff. He was the maternal great grandfather of US President **JOHN F. KENNEDY**.

RICHARD HARRIS is best known for his roles as King Arthur in *Camelot* and Albus Dumbledore in the first two *Harry Potter* films.

The De Valera Museum and Bruree Heritage Centre uses audio-visuals and memorabilia to tell the story of former President and Taoiseach **ÉAMON DE VALERA**.

BALLYHOURA MOUNTAINS

GALTEE MOUNTAINS

Two boys, digging in a potato field near Ardagh in 1868, discovered **THE ARDAGH CHALICE**. It is now in the National Museum.

The highest point of the county is **CAIRN HILL**. It is the site of a big television transmitter broadcasting to much of the Irish midlands.

The **AUGHNACLIFFE DOLMEN** has a delicately balanced top stone. It is around 5,000 years old. The dolmen in Aughnacliffe gives the townland its name: 'The Field of the Stones'.

The **OLD CORN MILL** in Drumlish was used for the milling of oats into oatmeal and also for corn-crushing. It helped sustain people during the famine.

RIVER SHANNON

ST MEL'S CATHEDRAL in Longford can be seen from a long way outside the town. There is a museum situated at the rear of this cathedral.

LOUGH FORBES

The Johnny Keenan **BANJO FESTIVAL** held in Longford town in September celebrates Irish traditional music along with American bluegrass and folk music.

LOUGH REE

LONGFORD TOWN

EDDIE MACKEN, the Olympic showjumper, was born in Granard in Longford.

The **ROYAL CANAL** is navigable from Dublin to Abbeyshrule. The canal is used for boating, fishing, walking and nature study.

The **TALLEST TREE** in Longford is a Sitka spruce at Castle Forbes, Newtownforbes. It is 38.5 metres tall!

OLIVER GOLDSMITH

was a novelist, playwright and poet believed to be from Longford. He is best known for his novel *The Vicar of Wakefield*. He is credited with writing the classic children's tale *The History of Little Goody Two-Shoes*, the source of the phrase 'goody two-shoes'.

LONGFORD
-- Longfort --

GRANARD TRADITIONAL HARP FESTIVAL

is a celebration of the music of the harp with competitors coming from all over Europe.

GLEN LOUGH

Nature Reserve is an area of special protection. It has a large number of whooper swans during wintertime and is home to lots of different species of ducks, like the wigeon and teal.

The Abbeyshrule AIR SHOW is Ireland's longest-running air show. It features aircraft from the Irish Air Corps, US Air Force and some of the best civilian acts in Ireland and the UK!

There is a TITANIC MONUMENT and Garden in Ennybegs in memory of James Farrell for saving the lives of two girls on the sinking ship.

Longford has all the native Irish BUTTERFLY species including the clouded yellow, red admiral and painted lady.

LOUTH
An Lú

Louth is a setting in the **TÁIN BÓ CÚAILNGE** (The Cattle Raid of Cooley). In this story, the famous warrior Cúchulainn fought Queen Maeve of Connacht's whole army by himself to protect Ulster which was under a spell.

Co. Louth is named after Lugh, a god of ancient Ireland whose festival was celebrated at **LÚNASA** (beginning of autumn).

A tall **STANDING STONE** at Knockbridge is said to be the one Cúchulainn tied himself to as he was dying!

ST BRIGID is believed to have been born in Faughart in AD 451. There is a shrine to her there, with a path that leads to a well and a grotto.

The ruins of **KING JOHN'S CASTLE** tower above the harbour in Carlingford.

The world famous family band **THE CORRS** were brought up in Dundalk.

OLD MELLIFONT ABBEY was Ireland's first Cistercian monastery. Less than 30 years later it had 100 monks and 300 lay brothers. Today, the extensive remains include an unusual octagonal lavabo (wash room).

DERMOT O'BRIEN was a céilí band and showband musician as well as a Gaelic footballer!

For many years, the All-Ireland **POC FADA** competition has taken place on the Cooley Mountains. Poc Fada is a style of long-distance hurling!

CARLINGFORD LOUGH

COOLEY MOUNTAINS

St Peter's Church in Drogheda is world famous for housing the shrine of **OLIVER PLUNKETT**. His preserved head forms the centre piece of the shrine in the church!

DUNDALK

Carlingford **OYSTER** Festival is held every year in early August.

Baltray is home to a large colony of **LITTLE TERNS**. A project to protect the little terns is run by Louth Nature Trust.

THE ISLE OF MAN is just a 96 km sail away from Carlingford Lough!

ARDEE CASTLE is the largest fortified medieval tower house in Ireland!

RIVER BOYNE

MUIREDACH'S HIGH CROSS is the most richly decorated of its kind in Ireland.

Leading into Bellacorick you cross the **MUSICAL BRIDGE**. The stones on the sides of the bridge give out a sound when struck. Each block gives out a different note and when played together, they can form a tune!

The **CÉIDE FIELDS** are the remains of a Stone Age community which lived here in 3,000 BC! It is the oldest known farming community in the world.

INISHKEA ISLANDS

MOYNE ABBEY is one of the most impressive ecclesiastical ruins in Mayo. It was founded as a Franciscan friary.

MWEELREA MOUNTAIN is the highest point in the province of Connacht.

KILLALA is dominated by two towers: a round tower and St Patrick's Cathedral.

MARY ROBINSON was born in Ballina. She was the first female President of Ireland! In 2009 she was awarded the Presidential Medal of Freedom by the United States.

CASTLEBAR

BUNLAHINCH Clapper Footbridge is an ancient form of bridge. It is formed by large flat slabs of stone supported on stone pillars.

WESTPORT has been voted the best place to live in Ireland and has won the Tidy Towns competition many times over.

CLARE ISLAND

INISHBOFIN   INISHTURK

The **NATIONAL MUSEUM OF COUNTRY LIFE** near Castlebar has a large collection of objects which display how rural people used to live!

CROAGH PATRICK is considered the holiest mountain in Ireland. Pilgrimages to the mountain have been held since the Stone Age!

TOORMAKEADY is a Gaeltacht on the western side of Lough Mask.

LOUGH MASK

The **GAELTARRA KNITWEAR** factory is one of Údarás na Gaeltachta's many projects for boosting the local economy.

The **DOLMEN** of the Four Maols is named after the four Maol brothers who murdered a bishop. They were killed and buried near the dolmen.

River Moy

There are around 140 species of **BIRDS** that visit Mayo. Some of the rarer ones are the crossbill, whimbrel, water rail and red-breasted merganser.

Ireland West **AIRPORT** is 20 km outside Knock. It only has one runway!

Foxford has a thriving Woollen Mill and **FOXFORD BLANKETS** have a worldwide reputation for quality.

KNOCK is a religious shrine and place of pilgrimage, where it is claimed that there was an apparition of the Virgin Mary, St Joseph, St John, angels, a lamb and a cross on the wall of a church.

LOUGH CARRA is the largest marl (limestone) lake in Ireland!

The film **THE QUIET MAN** was partly filmed in Cong. There is a museum in the village which is dedicated to the film!

MICHAEL DAVITT is one of Mayo's heroes. He was a reformer, writer and politician who started the National Land League with C.S. Parnell to help people get rights to their own land!

MAYO
- Maigh Eo -

Over 90 monuments are located in the Brú na Bóinne (Palace of the Boyne) region of Meath, including the **KNOWTH AND DOWTH** passage tombs.

Meath has very good land and is Ireland's leading producer of **POTATOES**!

Kells is best known as the site of the Abbey of Kells, from which the **BOOK OF KELLS** takes its name.

Ireland's only **INLAND LIGHTHOUSE** is the Tower of Lloyd outside Kells. It was used to watch horseracing and take in the magnificent views!

The Megalithic Passage Tomb at **NEWGRANGE** was built about 3200 BC. The passage and chamber of Newgrange are illuminated by the winter solstice sunrise once a year!

RIVER BLACKWATER

Co. Meath has the only two **GAELTACHT** areas in Leinster: Baile Ghib and Ráth Cairn.

The comedian **TOMMY TIERNAN** is from Navan town!

NAVAN

The world famous **TARA BROOCH** was discovered on the beach in Bettystown. It is now kept in the National Museum of Ireland in Dublin.

ROYAL CANAL

The actor **PIERCE BROSNAN** grew up in Navan. He is best known for his role as James Bond in four films!

Teltown was home to Ireland's own pre-Olympic Games. These ancient Irish games became the **TAILTEANN** games and the sports included running, high-jumping, hurling, quoit throwing, wrestling, boxing and slinging contests!

The **NEWCASTLE LAKE** wildlife sanctuary is situated in the north of Meath. In summer the air buzzes with dragonflies.

MEATH
– An Mhí –

SLANE CASTLE is located in the town of Slane. The castle has been the home of the Conyngham family since the 18th century. Since 1981, the grounds of Slane Castle have been used to host rock concerts!

RIVER BOYNE

SIR FRANCIS BEAUFORT was born in Navan. He was the creator of the Beaufort scale which is how we measure wind force!

BELLEWSTOWN racecourse has two festivals every year. The races have always been associated with the smell of freshly mown hay and the taste of strawberries and cream!

There is a **CAR SHOW** held every year in Trim. It is where vintage cars and motorcycles are on show to be admired.

NAVAN is the county town of Meath and has one of the world's few palindromic placenames!

TAYTO

THE HILL OF TARA was the coronation place of Ireland's kings!

TAYTO PARK near Ashbourne is an exciting theme park and zoo!

The **BUFFALO RIDGE** at Tayto Park is home to Ireland's first herd of American Bison. Over 20 buffalo roam the plains at Tayto Park.

Co. Monaghan is called the **DRUMLIN COUNTY** because of its many drumlins, or rounded hills!

JUAN MACKENNA was born John MacKenna near Monaghan. He was a Chilean army officer and hero of the Chilean War of Independence!

The **FIDDLER OF ORIEL** competition is part of a traditional music festival held every May in Monaghan town.

MULLAN VILLAGE is a well-preserved industrial village. Mullan had a large flax mill and was at the centre of the linen industry in the 18th and early 19th centuries!

Edergole has a number of ringforts as well as Edergole Court Tomb, known locally as **THE GIANT'S GRAVE**.

PATRICK KAVANAGH, from Innishkeen, is regarded as one of the foremost poets of the 20th century. A local centre was established to commemorate the poet and writer.

MONAGHAN MUSHROOMS is one of the largest mushroom producers in the world!

CLONES began as a monastic settlement when St Tiernach founded his monastery there. The round tower there is 22 metres tall!

MONAGHAN
Muineachán

The comedian and actor **ARDAL O'HANLON** was born in Carrickmacross. He is best known for playing Father Dougal McGuire in the television series *Father Ted*.

RIVER BLACKWATER

SLIEVE BEAGH

COOLBERRIN HILL

ROSSMORE FOREST
Park is mainly deciduous with fine examples of beech, spruce, oak, ash and giant redwood!

MONAGHAN TOWN

Carrickmacross is well known for **CARRICKMACROSS LACE** which has a beautiful, individual style.

There is a **CAIRN** at the top of Mullyash! There is a clear view of this cairn from most of the megalithic tombs in east Monaghan. There was once a tradition of visiting the cairn on the last Sunday of July.

MONAGHAN COUNTY MUSEUM is one of the leading provincial museums in Ireland. Its most important exhibit has to be the Cross of Clogher, a processional cross dating from the 14th century.

LOUGH MUCKNO

MULLYASH MOUNTAIN

RIVER FANE

LOUGH EGISH is noted for its pike fishing.

The Irish **BOG SNORKELLING** Championships take place in Castleblayney each year. This is where you swim two lengths in a trench cut through a peat bog!

CARRICKMACROSS WORKHOUSE is a Community Resource, Training and Heritage Centre. It was one of 130 workhouses built between 1841 and 1843 to house the poor.

49

OFFALY
– Uíbh Fhailí –

The town of **HORSELEAP** got its name from an incident where someone had to flee the village and jumped his castle's moat on horseback!

Tullamore is the site of the world's first known aviation disaster! The town was damaged when a **HOT AIR BALLOON** crashed and caused a fire that burned down 130 homes!

RIVER BROSNA

GRAND CANAL

THE TULLAMORE SHOW is a one-day agricultural show held near Tullamore every year.

The River Shannon offers a good cross-section of the fauna of Ireland, including **BROWN HARES**!

21% of the land in Offaly is bogland!

Falmouth Kearney was a maternal great-great-great grandfather of **BARACK OBAMA**, the 44th President of the United States. He was from Moneygall and emigrated to New York in 1850.

RIVER SHANNON

MOUNT SAINT JOSEPH ABBEY is the home of a community of Cistercian monks. They run a dairy farm, a guesthouse and a boys boarding college!

milk

The **CLARA BOG** boardwalk is very popular. It allows walkers to safely cross the surface of the bog.

Birr was the site where certain galaxies were observed for the first time through the historic **BIRR TELESCOPE**. It was shaped like a canon and was the largest telescope in the world for 70 years!

BIRR CASTLE
has been the seat of the Parsons family, Earls of Rosse, for 14 generations. The Irish Game and Country Fair is held here every year.

TULLAMORE

Cloghan was once a great centre of trade and **ROMAN COINS** have been discovered throughout the town.

Birr Castle Estate is home to the largest **TREE HOUSE** in Ireland!

MICK

The **SLIEVE BLOOM MOUNTAINS** is one of the few remaining areas in Ireland where grouse is still a common bird in the summer!

KILLEIGH is the birthplace of the famous greyhound Mick the Miller. A statue has been placed on the village green to commemorate him.

Edenderry is the home of the Irish **PARACHUTE** Club. They train and provide facilities for skydiving enthusiasts and for charities.

'WELL, THAT BEATS BANAGHER' is a well-known phrase. It dates from the 19th century when Banagher was the worst example of a 'rotten borough'. If something 'beats Banagher' it must be very bad indeed!

LEAP CASTLE is one of the most haunted castles in Ireland! Lights can be seen in the castle at night.

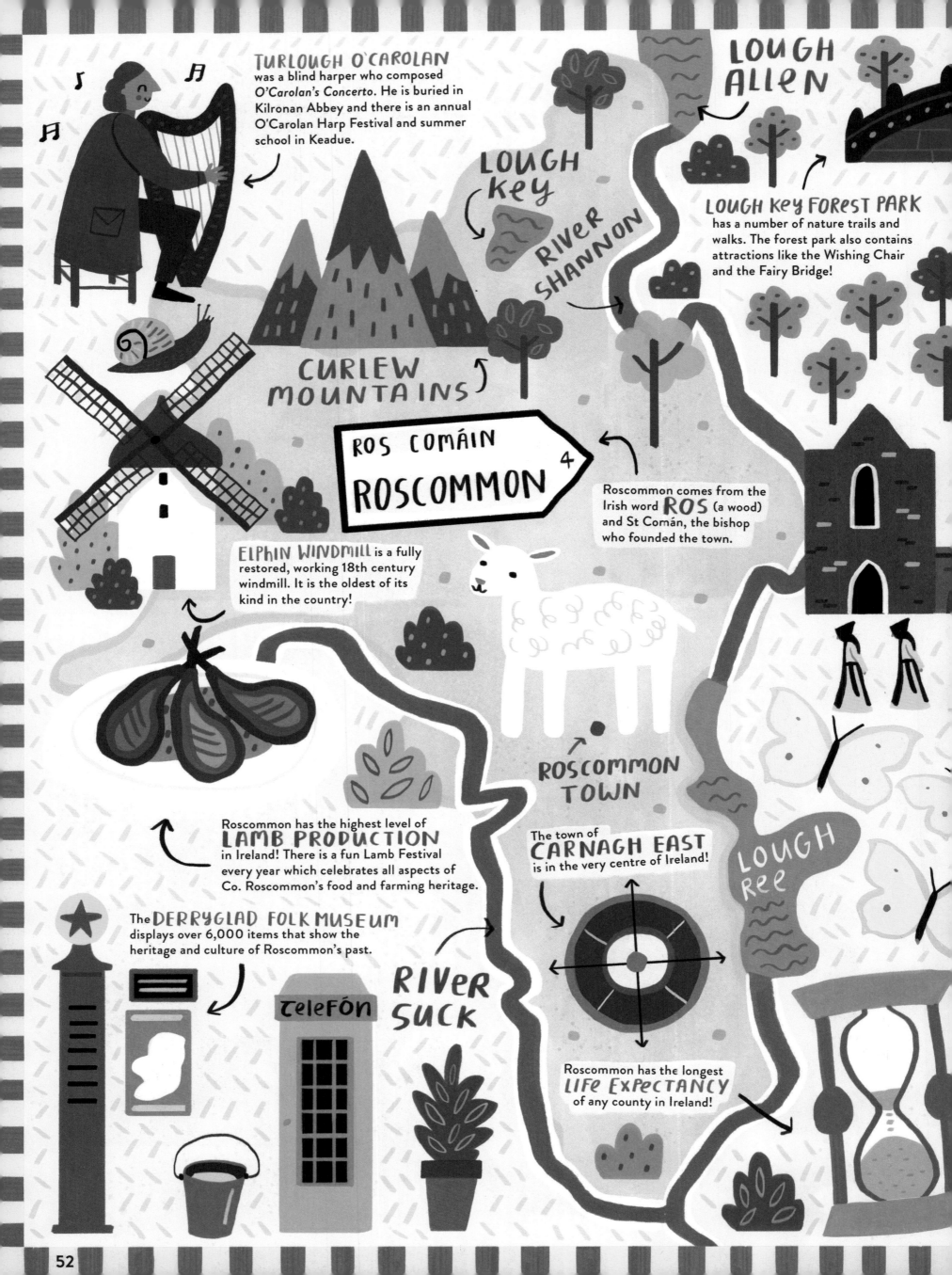

TURLOUGH O'CAROLAN was a blind harper who composed *O'Carolan's Concerto*. He is buried in Kilronan Abbey and there is an annual O'Carolan Harp Festival and summer school in Keadue.

LOUGH KEY

LOUGH ALLEN

RIVER SHANNON

LOUGH KEY FOREST PARK has a number of nature trails and walks. The forest park also contains attractions like the Wishing Chair and the Fairy Bridge!

CURLEW MOUNTAINS

ROS COMÁIN
ROSCOMMON

Roscommon comes from the Irish word **ROS** (a wood) and St Comán, the bishop who founded the town.

ELPHIN WINDMILL is a fully restored, working 18th century windmill. It is the oldest of its kind in the country!

ROSCOMMON TOWN

Roscommon has the highest level of **LAMB PRODUCTION** in Ireland! There is a fun Lamb Festival every year which celebrates all aspects of Co. Roscommon's food and farming heritage.

The town of **CARNAGH EAST** is in the very centre of Ireland!

LOUGH REE

The **DERRYGLAD FOLK MUSEUM** displays over 6,000 items that show the heritage and culture of Roscommon's past.

TELEFÓN

RIVER SUCK

Roscommon has the longest **LIFE EXPECTANCY** of any county in Ireland!

ROSCOMMON
— Ros Comáin —

The famous actor **CHRIS O'DOWD** was born in Boyle!

Near Rathcroghan is **OWEYNAGAT** (Cave of the Cats). It is also known as the 'entrance to the Otherworld', where magical creatures emerge from!

BOYLE ABBEY is an impressive and well-preserved Cistercian Monastery which was founded by the MacDermot family.

For 300 years, iron and coal were the mainstay of industry in Arigna. The **MINER'S WAY** trail follows many of the paths used by miners going to work in the Arigna Mines.

The **BRIMSTONE BUTTERFLY** is widespread in Roscommon. It lays its eggs on the leaves of the buckthorn tree.

One-third of the population of Roscommon was lost during the Famine. The Irish National **FAMINE MUSEUM** in Strokestown is located in the original stable yards of Strokestown Park House to remember those years.

SLIGO
Sligeach

The sandy beach at Streedagh is the resting place of three ships and 1,800 men from the SPANISH ARMADA.

INNISHMURRAY contains the remains of an early Christian monastery founded by St Molaise!

SLIGO TOWN

The YEATS MEMORIAL BUILDING in Sligo town commemorates the work of William Butler Yeats.

MULLAGHMORE is one of the best big wave surfing locations in the world.

Neil JORDAN, filmmaker and novelist, was born in Sligo. He directed many famous films, including Michael Collins, The Crying Game and The Company of Wolves.

SLIGO ABBEY was built in the 1200s. It has a great wealth of carvings including Gothic tomb sculpture. There is a well-preserved cloister there and a sculptured altar.

OX MOUNTAINS

BRICKLIEVE MOUNTAINS

Three members of the successful boyband WESTLIFE (Kian Egan, Mark Feehily and Shane Filan) were born in Sligo.

EAGLES FLYING is a bird-watching attraction in Sligo where you can see huge birds of prey flying right over your head.

The LILY LOLLY CRAFTFEST is a celebration of the legacy of Susan and Elizabeth Yeats, sisters of William Butler Yeats, affectionately known as Lily and Lolly.

DOLLY'S COTTAGE is a 200-year-old, traditional thatched cottage. It is the only one of its kind in the area and is open to the public during the summer.

BENBULBIN is a large rock formation that is part of the Dartry Mountains. It is said to be the resting place of Diarmuid and Gráinne, the mythical couple.

DARTRY MOUNTAINS

PAULINE McLYNN is an actress and author who was born in Sligo. She is best known for her role as the tea-loving Mrs Doyle in *Father Ted*!

LOUGH GILL

Sligo is often called **YEATS COUNTRY**. The playwright and poet William Butler Yeats and his brother, artist Jack Butler Yeats, spent many childhood holidays here. William wrote many poems about the county.

The 17th-century **PARKES CASTLE** is on the banks of Lough Gill. The castle has been fully restored using Irish oak and traditional craftsmanship.

CONSTANCE MARKIEVICZ, the nationalist, suffragette and socialist, grew up in Lissadell. She was one of the first women in the world to hold a cabinet position.

CARROWMORE Megalithic Cemetery is the largest megalithic site in Ireland and among the oldest in Europe! There are over 60 tombs here. The oldest tomb here is even older than the Egyptian Pyramids!

LOUGH ARROW

The **MERMAID STONES OF SCURMORE** is a mound with six stones on top. Apparently, a chieftain saw a mermaid and removed her powers so she could not return to the sea. He married her and they had seven children. She recovered her powers eventually and went back to the sea, but she turned six of her children to stone and took the youngest one with her.

CURLEW MOUNTAINS

BIRDWATCHERS are very active in Sligo because there are many beautiful birds that can be spotted across the county, like storm petrels, choughs and the occasional black-throated diver.

In 1865, the Dundrum **METEORITE** landed in a potato field in Clonoulty!

LOUGH DERG

The LIFE & OPINIONS OF TRISTRAM SHANDY, GENTLEMAN

LAURENCE STERNE from Clonmel is best known for his novel *The Life and Opinions of Tristram Shandy, Gentleman*.

SILVERMINE MOUNTAINS

NENAGH

DERRYNAFLAN monastery became famous when a hoard of 8th-century treasure was found there in 1980. The Derrynaflan Hoard is on display in the National Museum of Ireland in Dublin.

RIVER NORE

Tipperary is famous for its horse-breeding industry. It is home to **COOLMORE STUD**, the headquarters of the world's largest breeding operation of thoroughbred racehorses.

BULMERS CIDER and **CIDONA** both originated in Clonmel! Bulmers is still made in Tipperary using traditional ingredients and methods.

The imposing **CAHIR CASTLE** was the scene of sieges for hundreds of years. It was built in such a way that makes it look like it is growing from the rock it sits on!

RIVER SUIR

The **SWISS COTTAGE** in Cahir is an 'ornamental cottage'. It was originally built for entertaining the guests of Lord and Lady Cahir!

GALTEE MOUNTAINS

Thurles is the birthplace of the Gaelic Athletic Association. The GAA was founded in 1884 at a meeting in **HAYES HOTEL**.

The crosses of **AHENNY** are probably the earliest group of ringed high crosses in Ireland.

TIPPERARY CRYSTAL produces crystal, glassware, cutlery and ceramics.

KNOCKMEALDOWN MOUNTAINS

Local legend has it that a king lived in **LOUGHMORE CASTLE** and offered his daughter's hand in marriage to whoever could kill a gigantic boar that lived nearby. The area is known as 'the Field of the Reward' because of this story!

Ballyporeen is best known for being the ancestral home of United States former President **RONALD REAGAN**.

TIPPERARY
- Tiobraid Árann -

The **ROCK OF CASHEL** was said to be formed when Satan took a bite from the Devil's Bit mountain and spat the rock away! The group of buildings on the rock is one of the best examples of Celtic art and medieval architecture in Europe!

Cahir was one of the first towns in Ireland to be serviced by **STAGECOACH** in the 19th century! Charles Bianconi set up the coach services between Clonmel, Cahir and Cashel.

THE CLANCY BROTHERS were an influential folk band who were very popular in the 1960s. They released more than twenty albums and were from Tipperary!

H₂O   uisce   WATER

TIPPERARY NATURAL **MINERAL WATER** has its source in the village of Borrisoleigh, and was Ireland's first bottled natural mineral water!

CASHEL BLUE farmhouse cheese is an internationally renowned blue cheese which is made near Fethard!

PAT SHORTT, the actor and comedian, was born in Thurles!

TYRONE
– Tír Eoghain –

BRIAN FRIEL, the playwright, was born in Tyrone. He has written more than 30 plays. Two of his best known are *Philadelphia, Here I Come!* and *Dancing at Lughnasa*.

The emblem of Tyrone GAA is a **RED HAND**! The legend is that there was a race to decide who would be king of Ulster. One of the contenders was losing so he cut off his hand and flung it across the winning line before his rival could reach it!

GRAY, PRINTER

STRABANE was once a centre of the printing industry. Gray's Printing Press is an 18th-century printer that is still in use today. James Wilson, Woodrow Wilson's grandfather, was an apprentice at Gray's!

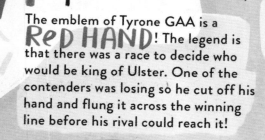

Lots of unique flora grow in Tyrone, including **CLOUDBERRY** and **EARLY PURPLE ORCHID**.

The professional golfer **DARREN CLARKE** is from Dungannon!

The **GORTIN GLEN** Forest Park is an area of natural beauty which is ideal for hiking and orienteering.

OMAGH

Brian O'Nolan, the novelist, playwright and satirist, is from Strabane. He wrote under the name **FLANN O'BRIEN**.

There is a glass memorial in **OMAGH** which pays tribute to the victims of the 1998 Omagh car bombing. Twenty-nine people died and 220 were injured from the terrible attack.

Castlederg hosts a traditional **APPLE FAIR** every year where apple growers go to sell their produce!

BACON CURING is one of the main industries in Tyrone today!

Two presidents of the USA, **ULYSSES S. GRANT** and **WOODROW WILSON**, have ancestral roots in Co. Tyrone!

SAWEL is the highest peak in Tyrone!

SPERRIN MOUNTAINS

The **GOLES STONE ROW** consists of eleven stones in a straight line. The stones date back to the Bronze Age when they were used for moon rituals.

Both **COAL** and **GOLD** have been mined in Tyrone, as well as the byproducts of silver and lead!

Cookstown has the longest street in Northern Ireland. It is known as **ONE MILE STREET**.

LOUGH NEAGH

RIVER BLACKWATER

WELLBROOK BEETLING MILL is an 18th-century water-powered mill that was once used in the production of linen. 'Beetling' is where the fabric is beaten with heavy weights which produce a glaze.

ST PATRICK'S CHAIR AND WELL in Altadaven Wood is said to have healing properties. Locals say that if you sit in the chair and make a wish, it will come true! The well is supposed to be good at healing warts.

Tyrone is the **BIGGEST** county in Northern Ireland!

ARBOE OLD CROSS is a 10th-century national monument which is believed to be the first high cross of Ulster!

Well GIRL! Well BOY!

The Waterford phrase **WELL** can mean both 'Hello' and 'How are you?'

RIVER SUIR

COMERAGH MOUNTAINS

People can fly to different cities in England from **WATERFORD AIRPORT.**

JOHN O'SHEA, from Ferrybank, has played for Manchester United and Sunderland. He has also been Captain of the Republic of Ireland team.

MONAVULLAGH MOUNTAINS

KNOCKMEALDOWN MOUNTAINS

Thomas Francis Meagher raised the first Irish **TRICOLOUR** in Waterford City in 1848.

RIVER BLACKWATER

SEAN KELLY, one of cycling's greats, was the World Number One cyclist for six years!

LISMORE CASTLE is the birthplace of Robert Boyle, the 'Father of Modern Chemisty'.

AN RINN is a Gaeltacht that's best known for its Irish college. During the summer, young people go there to improve their spoken Irish.

The round tower in **ARDMORE** was built by St Declan. Legend has it that he put a golden bell out to sea on a stone and followed it until it landed in Ardmore, where he built his monastery!

Waterford people eat **BLAAS** (white, floury bread buns) for breakfast or lunch. They are often served with **RED LEAD** (luncheon sausage).

In Waterford, a slingshot is called a **GALLYBANDER** and a snail is called a **SHELLAKYBOOKY**!

FISH, such as trout, sea trout and salmon, can be found in the Suir and the Blackwater.

WILLIAM JACOB began producing biscuits in Waterford in 1851. Jacob's were the very first manufacturers of cream crackers!

JACOB'S

SPRAOI is a summer street arts festival with a terrific fireworks display.

REGINALD'S TOWER is a defence tower from the 13th century. It is Waterford's most recognisable landmark and now houses an exhibition on Viking Waterford.

WATERFORD CITY

ERNEST WALTON, from Dungarvan, was a physicist and Nobel laureate. He was the first person, along with John D. Cockcroft, to artificially split the atom!

COUMSHINGAUN is a fine example of a corrie lake. This is a type of lake formed in the hole left by a glacier, which is then filled with rainwater!

World-famous **WATERFORD CRYSTAL** glassware is made here in the 'Crystal County'.

TRAMORE is Waterford's favourite holiday resort. It has a huge amusement park and a 5 km beach with sand dunes!

RASHERS were developed in Waterford by Henry Denny in 1820.

The Tramore **METAL MAN** is a statue that warns ships away from dangerous rocks.

DUNMORE EAST is a beautiful fishing village and holiday resort by the sea.

Waterford City is the oldest city in Ireland. It was built by the **VIKINGS** in the year AD 914.

People go **WHALE WATCHING** off the coast of Waterford to see dolphins, fin whales and even humpback whales!

WATERFORD

The coast of Waterford is ideal for swimming, wind surfing, fishing, boating, sailing and **EXPLORING**!

- Port Láirge -

WestMeath
An Iarmhí

JOE DOLAN was a pop singer from Mullingar. He is widely regarded as one of the greatest stars to come out of the Irish showband era.

Some say there have been sightings of a **LAKE MONSTER** in Lough Ree!

JOHN JOE NEVIN, the Olympic super-featherweight boxer, was born in Mullingar.

MULLINGAR PEWTER revived pewter-making with their collections of figurines, watches and goblets. The history of pewter in Ireland goes back over 800 years!

TULLYNALLY CASTLE was originally built in the mid 1650s. It is the largest castle in Ireland that is still used as a family home!

ROYAL CANAL

The HILL OF UISNEACH was once considered the centre of Ireland. On the hill are the remains of circular enclosures, barrows, cairns, a holy well and two ancient roads!

LOUGH REE

ATHLONE TOWN

SEAN'S BAR in Athlone is the oldest pub in Ireland and has been listed in the Guinness World Records for being the oldest pub in Europe!

LILLIPUT HOUSE was used by Jonathan Swift as a holiday home. The area was initially known as Nure but after the publication of *Gulliver's Travels*, locals began to call it Lilliput and the name stuck!

KNOCKBODY WOOD is inhabited by wild pheasant and is a popular attraction for local pheasant hunters.

RIVER SHANNON

LOUGH SHEELIN

MULLAGHMEEN is the highest hill in Westmeath but the lowest county top in the country!

THE CHILDREN OF LIR, the famous myth, took place on Lough Derravaragh. Lir's wife Aoife cursed his four children, and they were forced to live as swans for 300 years on the lake!

Mullaghmeen has the largest **BEECH** forest in Ireland!

Mullingar is famous for high-quality **BEEF**. The phrase 'beef to the heels like a Mullingar heifer' is a phrase used to describe somebody's strong legs!

LOUGH LENE

LOUGH DERRAVARAGH

LOUGH OWEL

RIVER BROSNA

FORE VALLEY is said to have seven wonders. For instance, St Fechin's Well is filled with water that will not boil. Nearby is a tree adorned with jewellery and rubbish that apparently does not burn, and a river that flows uphill!

NIALL HORAN, one of the singers in the boyband One Direction, is from Mullingar.

MULLINGAR

LOUGH ENNELL

BELVEDERE HOUSE was originally built as a hunting and fishing lodge for Robert Rochfort. The estate has a walled garden, parklands and an apiary (a beekeeping yard).

Robert Rochfort, known as 'The Wicked Earl', built a huge wall to block the view of his brother's more impressive house next door – this is called **THE JEALOUS WALL**!

BROWN TROUT and pike are both found in Lough Ennell, where fishing is very popular. One of Ireland's biggest ever brown trout was caught here in 1894!

WeXFORD
– Loch Garman –

The **SHELL COTTAGE** in Cullenstown was designed by Kevin Ffrench, who decorated his entire cottage with shells!

Seals, dolphins and whales can be seen from the Hook Peninsula, including the giant **HUMPBACK WHALE**!

RISSOLES are eaten across Wexford. These fried potato cakes are either battered or breadcrumbed and are normally served in chip shops.

The author **EOIN COLFER** was born in Wexford. He is best known for writing the Artemis Fowl science fiction series.

ARTEMIS FOWL

KILMORE QUAY holds a seafood festival every summer with road races, seafood cooking demonstrations and market stalls.

LOFTUS HALL is one of the most haunted places in Ireland. The devil is said to have visited the hall during a storm. When the family discovered his cloven feet, he left by flying through the ceiling. Apparently, the hole he left in the roof could never be repaired!

John F. Kennedy **ARBORETUM** near New Ross is a plant collection that contains 4,500 types of trees and shrubs from all around the world.

10,000 Greenland white-fronted **GEESE** come to the southeast of Wexford each winter. That's one-third of the entire world's population!

Beaches in Curracloe were used to film some scenes from the Oscar-winning movie **SAVING PRIVATE RYAN**.

Arthur Leared, a doctor from Wexford, invented the binaural **STETHOSCOPE** in 1851. Before this, stethoscopes only had one earpiece!

RIVER SLANEY

MOUNT LEINSTER is the highest point in Wexford.

BLACKSTAIRS MOUNTAINS

1 km

Wexford **STRAWBERRIES** are famous for their flavour. During the summer, they can be bought in shops and at wayside stalls!

BALLYTEIGUE has one of the best sand dune systems in Europe, which is over 9 km long.

RIVER BANN

Wexford is a great producer of **CHEESE**! Wexford cheddar and Carrigbyrne farmhouse cheese are two of the county's dairy exports.

The Irish National Heritage Park in **FERRYCARRIG** walks you through the history of Ireland since the Stone Age! You can visit a crannog, a fulacht fiadh, prehistoric houses and much more!

RIVER BARROW

The **DUNBRODY FAMINE SHIP** in New Ross is a replica of the emigrant ship that brought people from Ireland to North America during the famine.

WEXFORD TOWN

LADY'S ISLAND LAKE

There is a busy ferry service in **ROSSLARE** where passengers and vehicles can travel to Wales and France.

In the summer, Lady's Island Lake is an important breeding site for terns, especially the **ROSEATE TERN**.

YOLA is an extinct dialect of English once spoken in parts of Wexford.

HOOK HEAD has the oldest operating lighthouse in the world!

The **MOUNT USHER** Gardens are in Ashford on the outskirts of Wicklow town. It contains trees and shrubs from all over the world.

RIVER LIFFEY

POWERSCOURT HOUSE has beautiful walled gardens. It has been often used as a filming location because of its stunning façade.

On a clear day you can see Wales from the top of the Great **SUGARLOAF**.

TARA'S PALACE Museum of Childhood has a collection of antique toys from up to 300 years ago. One of the pieces is called Tara's Palace, an antique doll house with 22 rooms!

RIVER SLANEY

CLAY PIGEON shooting is a popular pastime that's enjoyed across Wicklow!

EDDIE JORDAN, the former racing driver and Jordan Grand Prix founder, grew up in Bray.

RUSSBOROUGH HOUSE is a stately house near Blessington. It is the longest house in Ireland!

DARA Ó BRIAIN, the comedian and television host, was born in Bray.

WICKLOW
— Cill Mhantáin —

POULAPHOUCA RESERVOIR is known locally as Blessington Lakes. The reservoir was created when the River Liffey was dammed to build a hydroelectric plant in the 1930s and 1940s.

THE WICKLOW MOUNTAINS

LUGNAQUILLA is the highest peak in the Wicklow Mountains!

BLESSINGTON LAKES

ARDMORE STUDIOS in Bray is Ireland's biggest film studio. My Left Foot, Braveheart and Excalibur were all made here!

GLENDALOUGH is home to a monastic site around the lake which was founded by St Kevin.

WICKLOW GAOL is said to be haunted! Some people claim to have had their hair pulled and to have seen the ghost of a little girl in the schoolroom!

CLARA LARA is an activity park that has been running since 1971. It has water slides, tree houses and Tarzan swings!

WICKLOW TOWN

AVOCA MILL

AVOCA is well known for its handweaving. The Avoca Mill is the oldest weaving mill in Ireland!

KATIE TAYLOR, the Irish, European, World and Olympic boxing champion, was born in Bray.

The **NINETEEN ARCHES** Bridge in Arklow is the longest handmade stone bridge in Ireland!

BRITTAS BAY is a busy summer holiday destination, especially with Dubliners. The beach is often used for kiteboarding and camping!

CYCLE POLO was invented in Wicklow in 1891!

CHARLES STEWART PARNELL, one of the greatest leaders of modern Irish history, was born in Rathdrum. The Parnell National Memorial Park is dedicated to his memory.

IN THE AIR

Common Blue Butterfly

Wood Pigeon

Barn Owl

Oystercatcher

Chaffinch

Tortoiseshell Butterfly

Black Headed Gull

Rook

Aer Lingus

Garden Tiger Moth

Blue Tit

Blackbird

Sparrowhawk

Swallow

Canada Goose

Fulmar

Buzzard

Cormorant

Brimstone Butterfly

Red Admiral Butterfly

Kittiwake

Robin

Tufted Duck

Pheasant

Large White Butterfly

Gannet

Mallard

White Ermine Moth

Peregrine Falcon

Orange Tip Butterfly

Jay

Peacock Butterfly

Song Thrush

Grey Heron

Puffin

Kestrel

Herring Gull

Ryanair

Mute Swan

Kingfisher

Shelduck

Orca / Killer Whale

Blue Shark

Tuna

Cockles

Lobster Pot

Mackerel

Cod

Lobster

Frog

Leatherback Turtle

Haddock

Frogspawn

Hake

Oyster

Jellyfish

Periwinkle

Sperm Whale

Salmon

Herring

Fishing Boat

Mussels

Crab

Conger Eel

Plaice

Prawn

Cuttlefish

Red Gurnard

Harbour Porpoise

Currach

Skate

Trout

Basking Shark

Grey Seal

IN THE WATER

Bank Vole

Helicopters

Sycamore Tree

Hedgehog

Yew Tree

Pipistrelle Bat

Brown Rat

Daddy Longlegs

Ash Tree

Badger

Fallow Deer (Doe)

Elder Tree

Grey Squirrel

Rowan Tree

Horse Chestnut Tree

Stoat

Conkers

Feral Goat

Ivy

Rabbit

House Spider

Field Mouse

Bay Willow Tree

ON THE LAND

Red Squirrel

Oak Tree

Shrew

Common Lizard

House Mouse

Fox

Hawthorn Tree

Hazel Tree

Bracken

American Mink

Otter

Garden Slug

Blackthorn Tree

Red Deer (Stag)

Clover

Buttercup

Irish Hare

Garden Snail

Brown Lemonade

Red Lemonade

Full Irish Breakfast

Football Special

Barmbrack

KING

King Crisps

Curly Kale

Lamb Stew

Turnip

Rock Shandy

Billy Roll Ham

club

Breakfast Roll

Potato Farl

Colcannon

Ritchie's Mints

Tayto Crisps

TAYTO

MOO

Crisp Sandwich

Bacon and Cabbage

Parsnips

Klipso Bar

Spiced Beef

Macaroon Bar

Crubeens

Potatoes

Soda Bread

Mikado Biscuits

Rhubarb

Kimberley Biscuits

Seafood Chowder

Jambon

Black Pudding

White Pudding

Cabbage

Tea

WHAT WE EAT

Sliabh

Muc

Eala

Deilf

Sútha Talún

Prátaí

Gliomach

Coill

Eitleán

Damhán Alla

Líomanáid

Madra Rua

Mála Tae

Bainne

Fia

Féileachán

Seilide

Sliogáin

Camán

FOCLÓIR

Uachtar Reoite

Slisíní

Caisleán

Mainistír

Reilig

Cláirseach

Arán

Sráidbhaile

Abhainn

Droichead

Bratach

Sútha Craobh

Muileann Gaoithe

Luch

Ispíní

Cáis

Colúr

Cnónna

Teach Solais

Luamh

Oileán

Tarracóir

Fiddle

Tin Whistle

A seisiún is a gathering of musicians and singers who perform traditional Irish music for fun!

Uilleann Pipes

Irish Harp

Irish Dancing

Button Accordian

MUSIC & DANCE

A HAON

A DÓ

A TRÍ

Concertina

Irish Bouzouki

Mouth Organ (Harmonica)

The Spoons

Sean-nós Dancing

Bodhrán

Wooden Flute

THINGS WE DO

We play rounders.

We play road bowling, especially in Armagh and Cork.

Strawboys show up to weddings in the West. They wear straw masks and dance with the female guests!

We take down our decorations on 'Little Christmas' (January 6th).

We carve faces into turnips and eat monkey nuts for Samhain, or Halloween.

We make oat cakes and weave crosses on St Brigid's Day (February 1st).

We support our national team, no matter what the occasion!

#1

We play Gaelic Football.

We drink flat 7up when we're sick.

GRAFTON STREET

People from the country travel to Dublin to do their Christmas shopping on December 8th every year!

On December 26th, Wren Boys go around the houses collecting money for a party in their town!

We love to watch the Eurovision Song Contest!

We play hurling.

We leave a candle on the windowsill on Christmas Eve to welcome travellers.

We stay up late to watch *The Late Late Toy Show.*

We go for madcap swims on Christmas Day and New Year's Day.

We have big parades to celebrate St Patrick's Day (March 17th).

We play handball.

Horsebox

Pig (Sow and Bonhams)

Hereford Bullock (Beef)

Rooster

Bee

Combine Harvester

Rapeseed

Slurry Tank

Sheep

Shears

Wheat

Wellies

Trough

ON THE FARM

Hay Bales

Hay Barn

Bronze Turkey

Electric Fence

Friesian Cow (Dairy)

Oats

Tractor

Chick

Hen

Toggenburg Goat

Eggs

Aylesbury Duck

Sheepdog

Embden Goose

Maize

Barley

Sugar Beet

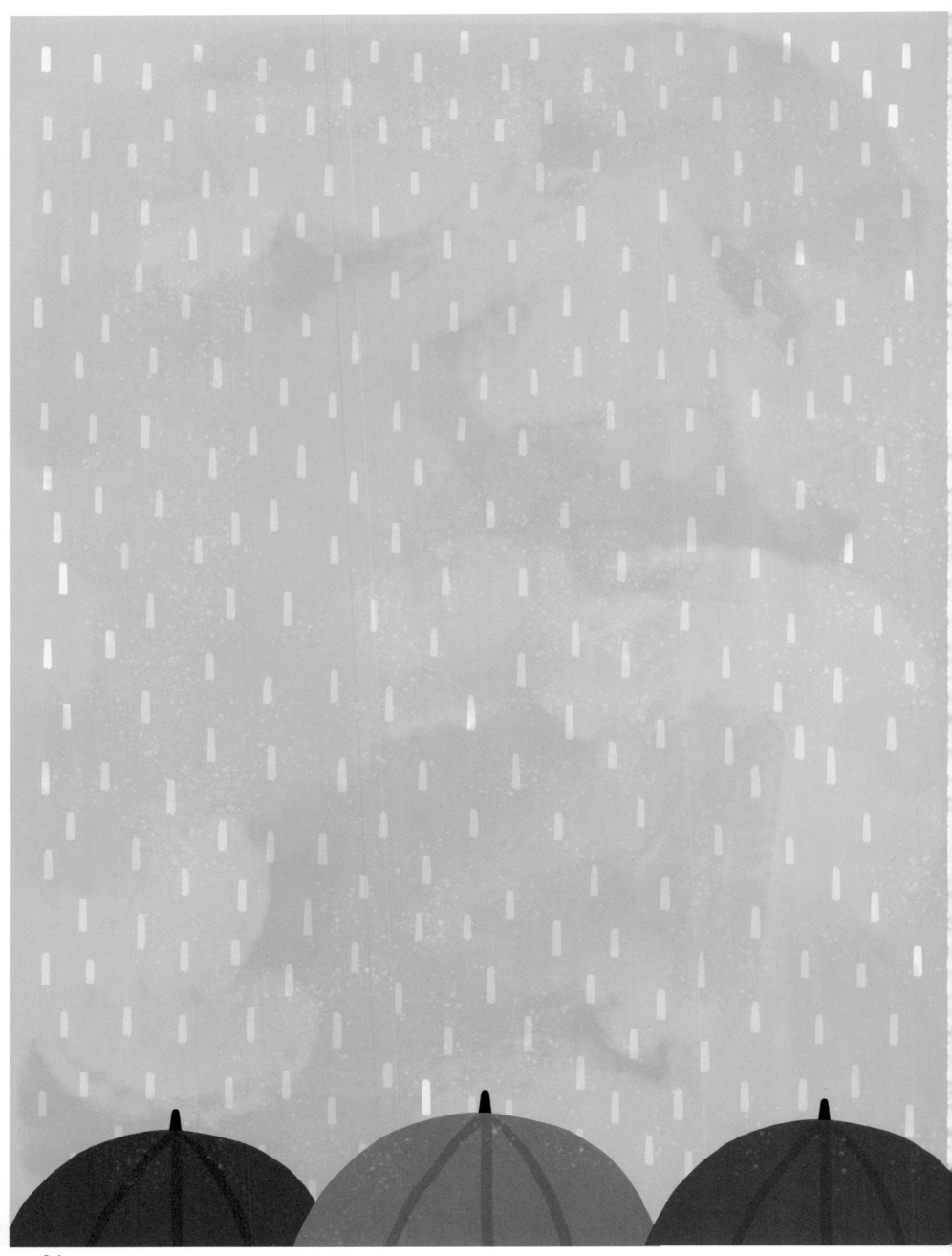

OUR WEATHER

INDEX

ABOUT *the* AUTHORS

Kathi 'Fatti' Burke is an illustrator with a passion for all things Irish. With a combined love of mapmaking and travel, she likes nothing more than drawing the places around her. She graduated from NCAD in 2012 and has been working as an illustrator ever since, creating commercial, editorial and commissioned pieces. Originally from Co. Waterford, Kathi now lives and works in Dublin City (which you can find on p. 2).

John Burke is a retired primary school teacher and was Teaching Principal of Passage East National School from 1980 to 2009. He has always been interested in environmental studies, local history and exploring Ireland. He is currently Chairperson of Waterford Teachers' Education Centre and Secretary of Barony of Gaultier Historical Society. He lives in Waterford (which you can find on p. 60). He is also Kathi's dad!

GILL BOOKS

Hume Avenue

Park West

Dublin 12

www.gillbooks.ie

Gill Books is an imprint of M.H. Gill & Co.

978 07171 6938 2

Indexed by Eileen O'Neill

Printed by G. Canale & C. S.p.A, Italy

This book is typeset in Brandon Grotesque Bold.

The paper used in this book comes from the wood pulp of managed forests. For every tree felled, at least one tree is planted, thereby renewing natural resources.

A CIP catalogue record for this book is available from the British Library.

10 9 8 7